# MEANT FOR EACH OTHER

COMPILED BY

## DEEPANSHI SHARMA

# MEANT FOR EACH OTHER

*Love is something in which two people hold each other tenaciously and their bond becomes inextricable.*

*TO LOVE AND BE LOVED IS THE GREATEST GIFT*

# Meant for each other

Birds were warbling in the lawn and a gardener was watering the plants and, in the meanwhile, Ava came and told the gardener to be careful with the roses as she had immense affection for roses. Suddenly she saw her son screaming and wincing in pain as he lost his balance while alighting the stairs and hit his toes. She rushed towards her son and started scolding him about his indolent and restless behaviour. The boy whose name was Mickel, was an obstinate boy. He was a nonchalant introvert who lacked interest in gelling up with people and did not want anyone to invade his privacy.

Ava prepared breakfast for Mickel and then she summoned him to come and have his food. Mickel ate slothfully, meanwhile, Ava was persistently observing him that how pathetically he was eating. She was brimming with anger, anyhow she tried to compose herself and advised him to act in polite and organized way. But as usual her all the counselling went flat on him and he then moved to his college. He was cycling to the college, then within few seconds, he realized that he is forgetting something. He held himself still and started ruminating on it. He opened his bag in order to check what was he missing, but the search came up with zilch. Afterwards, a ball hit on his head, then an epiphany stroke that he forgot his Physics book back at home. He returned to his home to get the book but at the same time the fear of getting scolded by his mother made him anxious. Anyways he strengthened his courage to enter the house. On the way, he saw the students going to the college, he murmured to himself, "what an awful start of the day!!!". When he went back to home & asked his mother whereabouts, his housemaid told him that his mother had some errands to run & she will be back soon. He rushed towards his room, looked for his book and carefully kept it in the bag.

On his way back to the college he somehow felt relieved, so he started humming his favorite songs, the zephyr adorned the pulchritude of the surroundings. Suddenly he saw a nicely dressed blue eyed girl with auburn hair came riding on her bicycle from the opposite end. Just her sight sent Mickel to frenzy and he was bewitched by her grace. He lost his balance and after a few seconds, their bicycles collided with each other and it just went out of blue. The collision made both of them reckless and impulsive.

The girl's dress was almost dishevelled which made her agitated and it seemed like that she was about to kill Mickel. Then the girl started screaming at him and said "are you blind"?  He too was ready to get into the altercation with her as he was having the bad day already. He replied, "didn't you see someone coming from the front". They kept on  squabbling which made the girl more irked, but she thought why she should waste her precious time with such imbecile person. Mickel was oozing with rage but he chose to keep quiet and let the girl speak as he was confined by his shyness.  After that, she gathered her stuff and moved towards the college by passing the comment "the nincompoop".

While Mickel was entering the college, he saw something lying on the floor which  looked more like a handkerchief that belonged to the girl. He took the handkerchief and opened it. As he opened it, one of his friends whose name was John arrived and told him that class is about to start. Then they both rushed to the classroom. On the way Mickel gave him a brief about his unpleasant start of the day, his dreadful encounter with the girl and how he ended up making her infuriated. Suddenly they both realized that their chit chat went for tad long and they had already missed their lecture. So now, they were sort of compelled to wait outside the classroom  for the next class as previous class was still in progress. Enjoying their usual banter, they discussed how they spent their weekends. John was a creative and a diligent student so he never let any weekend go unproductive. On the other hand, Mickel wickedly said how he spent the whole weekend doing absolutely nothing, when he recognized the same girl, he ran into this morning walking past them. Mickel tried to approach her but she disappeared at once. Then they both went to the canteen and ordered espresso and sandwiches for them. They were engrossed in their blathering so much so that they lost the track of time and in a that way they also missed the start of next lecture. John sighed 'WE ARE DOOMED MAN. This way we will end up missing all the lectures". We should at least give a try to enter the class. Mickel was reluctant to do so as his fragility suppressed him. For few seconds silence ensued and John forcefully took Mickel to the classroom by his arms.

In college, there was one austere teacher called Sophia who taught communication skills to the students. Students were scared of her.  Mickel and John were 15 minutes late to the class already. As a result, Sophia didn't allow them to attend the class and asked them to stay out of the class as punishment. A minute later the same girl Mickel had encounter with tried to enter the class. Mickel murmured to himself "Hell of a coincidence! This is the third time we are meeting today". He asked her with wavering voice 'Are you going to attend the class?"
 but he got no response from her. He asked again and beckoned to her by waving a handkerchief which drew Rose's attention towards him. She recognized that the handkerchief belonged to her and hated Mickel's action to keep her handkerchief sneakingly with him. She got irate and asked him where did he find her handkerchief but this time his ego didn't allow to respond in one go. He said to himself 'This is the taste of your own medicine girl". Without responding he returned her handkerchief. This abated ROSE's animus towards him and she murmured to herself 'Had I been too harsh on him? He isn't as halfwit as much he seems" she grinned. It seemed that both were ready to become friends. And then Mickel asked her that "What's your good name". She smoothly replied "Rose".

She further enquired "has the class started or do we still have few minutes left for the class"
 To which Mickel replied with a smirk on his face
'The class is yet to start. We must join it as today's class is really important Let's go". His assertive response sounded iffy to her. Little did she know about Mickel's intentions to avenge her by giving her a wrong idea so that she can get scolded by MISS SOPHIA to barge in the ongoing class without her permission.  John was astoundingly looking at Mickel and tried to fathom the fact that his dear friend could actually conspire against someone. The moment she opened the gate of the class, Mickel was on cloud nine as he was sure of Rose's humiliation in front of the class but to his surprise, the Miss Sophia let her attend the class.
Mickel cracked up and was gawking at the entrance gate of the class in bewilderment. They both pulled themselves together and decided to follow Rose so that they can get free pass to enter the class but as they entered in class  they both got reprimanded by Miss Sophia for entering behindhand in class without permission.At the same time, Mickel was looking for rose and was expecting her to get punished the same way as they were. His steady gaze raked over her which made her more agitated. As a consequence, they had to attend the whole lecture while standing.  Mickel had the bitter thoughts of self-reproach for his so far appalling day. "It would've been much better had I decided to stick to my bed all day long". He murmured to himself.

He saw ROSE in the corner of the class enjoying her lecture with utmost attention. This was exact opposite of what he thought would happen to Rose. All his efforts to avenge her went in vain. This further made him vexed with her.

At the break time, Mickel and his friend John were chilling in the canteen. John noticed that MICKEL was in pensive mood.
John asked him "What's bothering you pal? What are you musing over"?
To which MICKEL replied, "Don't you find it weird that Rose was allowed to enter the class while we weren't"? Why did she have that privilege? We all know it's impossible to be in good books of MS SOPHIA
JOHN replied "Get over it pal". You are just making yourself more anxious by indulging in futile thoughts". I knew you were trying to get even with her but please cut her some slack. Today was just not our day. Suddenly they both saw ROSE coming.
Rose came to them and said "I am here to extend my heartfelt gratitude to Mickel for returning me my handkerchief. You have no idea what it means to me." She said after I ran into you in the morning since then I have been looking for it & it was nowhere to be found. I was so distressed about it. Now that I have got it I am relieved. Mickel asked her 'why is it so precious to you'? She replied
  "IT was my father's present to me"
  MICKEL said ohhhh!!! and asked "what is his occupation?" Rose despondently said that "A year ago, he left for his heavenly adobe".

Mickel felt so sorry for her and tried to console her. John too said, "I am profoundly sorry for your loss". In these matters, Mickel was empathetic and sensitive. He said, "I can understand your feelings and emotions as my father is also no more." But there is no use to hold on to the past as it will bring back painful memories all we can do is to cherish the evocation of beautiful time that we had spent with them ". She said, "Separation is quite difficult and excruciating!!!". It is sometimes hard to believe that my father is no more. That whole situation became so poignant.

Next Day, it was Tuesday morning and as usual Ava went to his room to wake him up for the school. Ava  has always been concerned about his son as she knew she is the only one who takes care of him. Mickel slowly woke up and kept his head in her lap. He started telling yesterday's incident and how the day went against him and also about ROSE. Ava said, "I am glad that you found a new friend in your class!!!". Since, Mickel was an introvert so he didn't have any friends except John.
She further asked about her and her family. He described in candour, about her way of speaking, her auburn hair etc and etc…
While he was getting ready for his college, the thought of misinforming Rose about the commencing of class was constantly pestering him. He shouldn't have thought about the vengeance. These thoughts made him perplexed whether he should confess his erstwhile

intentions to her or not.

After that, he traditionally went to his college by his bicycle, and again saw ROSE. But this time there was no chaos, no disputes and no condemnation. Instead, both greeted each other and moved towards their college. On the way to the class, Mickel said "I wanted to confess one thing. She said what? He then replied that "I wanted to admit one thing that I purposely planned to send you to the class so that you can get punished the way I & JOHN both were for being late to the class."
She simply sniggered and said so you wanted to be on par with me as I was mean to you. He honestly said "ya!!! I apologize for what I did, but now we are good friends! Right?".  Silence ensued. He then asserted" Are we"??
Then she said "yeah!!, but it will take some time to strengthen our friendship!! and she further added that "English teacher is my mom" ….
This left him aghast and after all it's a big revelation for him. So, he took some time to digest the fact rose is a daughter of Miss Sophia.Now he realized why Rose was allowed to enter the class.
They talked for a while and parked their bicycles abreast. Then John accompanied both of them to the class.

**[scenario of a class]**
It was chemistry class, and the teacher was explaining a topic of organic chemistry
The majority of the class was yawning which

included Mickel as well. On the contrary, Rose was diligently listening to her

Just then teacher announced "all the students are supposed to perform the experiment in pairs. So all of you are expected to be present at laboratory where you will be performing the experiment on forthcoming Friday" After the announcement, there was a silent rush, everybody got busy in choosing his partner.

At the end of the class, the teacher also gave the assignments to the students which they were supposed to perform.

After the class Rose asked Mickel "Can we work together in the assignment"

 He surprisingly asked, "Which assignment?". She chuckled at the astonishment on his face and replied which was given by the chemistry teacher… were you not in class??

He then expressed his disinterest in chemistry. He replied" Chemistry is the subject I hate the most and specifically the reactions and structures. Rose replied in disagreement and articulated her love for chemistry by elaborating the importance of chemistry. The whole thing seemed mundane to Mickel, so he tried to change the topic

. He said that "you were talking about working in pair right'? I will be more than happy to join you as partner. This will improve my score. Rose smiled at him.

Mickel asked Rose "Will you be comfortable if we work on the assignment at my place" She hesitantly said "oK! I will come!!". In the evening, at 5 P.M. she visited Mickel's house. Ava opened the gate and welcomed ROSE. Ava

asked Rose about her hobbies and the goal of her life. Rose also asked in return about Ava's qualifications and in a way they both had a nice verbal confabulation.
In the meanwhile, Mickel came and introduced Rose to his mother. Then Ava said, ya! I know her now. We chatted too.
 You both can go ahead with your assignments. After that, they both headed towards the Mickel's room. They enjoyed their natter and discussed the assignment. After a while, Mickel started yawning and it seemed that soon he would drift away to sleep, Rose screamed to arouse him and said, "we need to make it to the top Mickel and for that, we have to put our every possible endeavour!!!". Mickel responded softly "OKay!". Rose was very competitive and always up for learning and implementing innovative things. By the end of the evening, they had discussed their ideas and evaluated the same

Next Day, Mickel asked her "would you mind if we go for a stroll in the evening?". She replied "sure!".
At 6 P.M. they both met in the central park and shared their likes and dislikes.
Both were enjoying swaying of the trees, blooming flowers in the sylvan surroundings and chirping of innocent birds. He has always been curious to know about her mother. He hesitatingly asked her how your relationship with your mother to which is she replied, "I have lost both the parents". Her wide stoic eyes were now brimming with tears. Mickel seemed

shocked to know that. She then said MS
SOPHIA is my stepmom. I lost my mother to
cancer after a long suffering. That was the worst
phase of my life, to realize and accept I'm losing
her year by year, bit by bit. To see her suffering
in excruciating pain shattered us both to the core.
Such amiable and cheerful soul was going to
leave us forever yet she fought her battle
courageously. All our prayers for her healthy
and long life went in vain and finally she
succumbed to her ailment and left both of us
alone… having said all this she started sobbing.
Tears started to roll down her cheeks. Mickel
wiped them with his hands. He could feel her
pain after all he had lost his father as well.
She then said My father married MISS SOPHIA
after a year my mother passed away, I got angry
at him at first and could not stop fretting over the
fact that he had given my mother's place to
another woman. How could he replace her so
easily? But life has its own course. It ambles by
no matter how hard you resist the change. I
made peace with him and MS SOPHIA. He had
his own life after all, and I did not want to be the
reason to ruin it. He had already suffered enough
and never lost his perseverance. He deserved a
life partner. MS SOPHIA was good wife but to
me she always seemed aloof. BUT I was
relieved to have my dad by my side. He never
neglected me, has always been there for me
through my thick and thin. I still remember the
most unfortunate day of my life when my world
turned upside down and I came to know that I

have lost my father forever in a car accident. I was crestfallen. To me that was the end of it. I did not have an iota of idea that GOD has such sort of plans for me. I was completely devastated. Within span of three years, I lost my world and MS SOPHIA is all I have for now. Mickel was in a dilemma. He could not figure what to say, how to console her. Her pain was way beyond his imagination. She kept mum for a while and said, "mom and dad used to look so perfect for each that other family members always adored them.I felt lucky to have such caring parents who lived for each other and for me ,but everything changed, EVERYTHING. HOW CAN LIFE BE SO UNFAIR ??SHE SAID WITH A PAINFUL SIGH.MICKEL HELD HER HANDS IS HIS and asked are you happy with Sophia. In response, she said, "Yes" in scepticism!!!Do I have another choice? At least there is someone back at home who cares whether I am alive or not. She is not that bad. We do not love each other but we try to get along. That's the best we can do to make each other's life simpler.

Then, he also told her about his father's generous and vibrant nature his intelligence and how he always encouraged and assisted him in her decisions. He was her mental emotional and academic support. His mind was as quick as computer, he used to solve maths puzzle and equations in a jiff. Rose and Mickel was reminiscing their parents. Both of them unified in their nostalgia with constant consolation from each side. ROSE then admitted to him "this is the first time I have ever vent my feelings out to someone. Whatever I have been through all these years I have kept them within myself. I have never had any friend, nor a mentor in which I can find momentary solace as fear of losing the person I can ever get near to always enshrouded my mind. I became introvert and aloof. Thanks for listening to me Mickel. She said with a smile

Mickel could resonate with her very well. He felt sorry to know how miserable she has been for such long years. A girl like her deserved so much but to her agony she hasn't got any care, love and condolence since long which was much needed. Mickel too had his experiences of loss but at least he had his mother with him. He suddenly realized that what having a mother by his side really means and to his mother's ordeal he has never been a good son to her. His way of dealing with his father's loss created a void between them. A feeling of guilt shrouded him. MICKEL wanted to hug ROSE but somehow restrained himself from doing so. He said thanks to ROSE for trusting him and ensured her that he will be always be there for her. This whole incident was an eye opener for MICKEL. Something inside him changed now.


On that day, at late-night Mickel suddenly woke up from slumber and was sweating profusely. He had a nightmare in which she saw Rose getting attacked by her mother. …". He called her in the midnight to make sure she is safe but the call went unanswered. The tension kept on intensifying. Anxiety and sense of impending doom began to enshroud him. Thereafter, there was a ping sound of notification, which led his momentary trepidation. He quickly checked; it was Rose. There was a state of stillness. He then checked the message anticipating everything would be alright at Rose's end.

 "I am sleeping, anything urgent!" Rose texted. He then took a sigh of relief. And he again went to hit the hay.

The next day the results of assignments were going to be announced. They both met at the entrance of the college gate making apprehensions of results. Rose was feeling bit nervous so Mickel tried to cheer her up. They headed towards their class.

The teacher quietly entered a class. There was pin-drop silence in the class that never happened before. The ambience of the class reflected a sense of disquietude.

The teacher was going to announce the results. Mickel and Rose were standing abreast.  Mickel was insouciant as usual as if he didn't care whatever the assessment would be, On the contrary, Rose was feeling peppy as well as overwrought.

The teacher announced, "Mickel and ROSE aced the results". Both of them felt exhilarated to know that. They both congratulated each other. Rose was on cloud nine and hugged Mickel in excitement which sent him to frenzy for a while. Somehow, he came back to his senses
& proposed the idea of celebrating their accomplishment… Rose said, "Yes! We should

definitely…, but where?". He said, "to our rendezvous."
She was bewildered and said, "what??". "The park!", he said.
She then exclaimed, "Oh!!" and corroborate for the same.
The next day, they both celebrated in the park along with their friends where John was also invited and some acquaintances of rose accompanied her. All of them congratulated Rose and Mickel. Among them, John brought graffe napoletane & tiramisu and Mickel brought cranberry juice. Rose served the juice to everybody. John spilt his juice on his Bermudas shorts as he got hit by the ball. This was the hilarious moment for everyone and Mickel started mocking him. Everyone was enjoying the party to the fullest.

 On the other side Mickel kept on thinking for having a moment alone with Rose a.  He wanted to confess his lingering feelings to Rose. Meanwhile he had no idea that how could he propose her, he didn't have the courage either. He began to think, about words and phrases he must use. Before proposing her, Mickel went to the corner of a park to practice what he would say. While practicing, he accidently bit his tongue. Anyhow he endured the pain and again started preparing himself to clear the test of love. Finally, his conscience gave him some kind of indication and then he mustered up his courage, took Rose in the lonesome corner of the park and confessed his feelings for her. For an instant, it seemed that she went into catatonic

stage.
But after a while, she pulled herself together
spurned his proposal and ran away from there.

 Mickel felt very distressed from the abrupt
reaction of Rose and was anxiously waiting for
the next day to confront her. He could feel his
heart aching  while wondering what on earth
has he done wrong! The feeling of angst
smothered him.

That night turned out horrible for him and a lot
of possibilities stroke him. He began to
contemplate what compelled Rose to refuse his
offer. Was it too soon for her? Does she have
someone special in her life already? Such
questions began to faze him. He anyhow
gathered his strength and laid on his bed but
couldn't sleep. HE kept tossing and turning in
his bed and was eagerly waiting to confront her
in the morning.

On  next day, he went to the college and
approached her in the entrance gate and asked
her "Why did you reject me? "Did I do
anything wrong?
She normally said", I shouldn't have behaved
this way please accept my apology but I cant
get in relationship with you as I am  already
engaged". I am sorry to hide this from you.
Mickel could see sorrow and pain in her eyes
He upsettingly said "OK!"
Then he asked "so can be become best friends!"
She said, "normal friends

Mickel felt relieved to have Rose as his friend.
With passing time their friendship grew
fonder. They assisted each other in homework,
shared their secrets. If one ever felt depressed
the other one has always been there to watch
others back.
After one month!
Ava went to his room to wake him up for his
college. He as usual woke up and got ready in
sluggish manner.
In college he was frantically looking for her, but
she was nowhere to be found
Then he asked one of her friends who told him
that Rose was absent. He was constantly
thinking why she didn't inform him as they used
to plan their day off together. He then thought to
ask Sophia, but he didn't congregate the courage
to ask.
In the evening, he tried to call Rose, but she didn't
pick neither of his call, nor did she replied to any
text which made him more perplexed.
Seven days had passed, still there was zilch
response from her. So Mickel decided to go to
her home and check what's wrong with her.
  He went to her place and rang the doorbell.
Miss Sophia opened the door and greeted him
He asked her about Rose.
Miss Sophia told him. 'Rose has got some
lurgy. I couldn't allow you to meet her but will
let her know that you came here to meet her.
Any message for her that you would like to
leave for her'?
Mickel was not convinced and was suspicious of
her intensions. He was determined to meet Rose
so he was looking for an excuse to enter the house

He replied "Now that I have come her, I have
some doubts regarding last class. Would you
mind solving them now" But as she was steadfast,
she denied and said "will discuss them in class.
You may leave now' with a wicked smile on her
face.
Mickel beseeched her to allow him to meet
Rose just for few seconds but all vent in
vain. At the end, he had to go as Rose's
mom was so adamant and didn't allow him
to meet her daughter. Mickel had to leave in
abounding disappointment.
His days and nights were passing in dismay.
He curled up in fear. His mind was
inundated with so much fear and nothing
could help ease his discomposure. He was
pondering what might could have happened
to her. He was constantly praying for her
safety.
That night, he was literally downhearted
and phrased his feelings in a poem,


Pain is invincible at times

That impedes us from sublime...

It implicitly extends the day

We are unable to find any ray...

It seems like it seizes

And it's gradually intertwined with our
memories...

It tempts us to fall in its trap

But eventually we find it all as crap...

It eats up all our strength

Which deteriorates our wavelength...

It amplifies our inner sentiments

Which deprives us from all the condiments...

It predominates on our every will

That makes our mastery swill...

Pain drags us down in the dumps

Invariably fabricating unhappy lumps...

It makes us languorous in all aspects

And impels to introspect...

Eventually, time does subside pain, but it does invoke at times

With alike intensity, it chimes...


But as Mickel wasn't more reluctant and reckless when it came to Rose. Next morning, he woke up with firm determination that he had to meet her no matter what it took. Mickel decided to approach Rose anyhow as he was so distressed and deliberate to know meet Rose and most importantly, to know the cause of this absurd discontinuity. He decided to approach Rose at night via her window.
He went to her home at night and was looking for a way to trespass .He didn't want to get

caught at any cost. Suddenly he heard a sound of footsteps and he ran away with aversion. He hid in the bushes of the garden so that he wouldn't get caught but unfortunately, he couldn't discover the way to Rose's room.

He was in a despondent state and was completely lost in his thoughts. He failed to meet ROSE that night too.

He became doleful and stopped interacting with his friends, even he didn't meet John for long. He couldn't eat and sleep which made his mother concerned for him. AVA asked him "what's wrong my son?". Then, he downheartedly told her everything. AVA tried to console him and advised him to be calm and unruffled. He began to lose his hope of meeting ROSE ever again.

One day, he was wandering in the park in melancholy, stared how children were playing joyfully and were enjoying their evening. He found Sophia in the park who was hanging out with her friends. He immediately ran towards ROSE'S house as this could be his only chance to meet her. JOHN asked him ,"Where are you off to ?",but he didn't reply. After reaching her house he recollected his breath and rang the doorbell. Rose opened the door and was awestruck when she saw him. Suddenly, she hugged him and started blubbering. He embraced her and calm her down.

She showed her rage and shouted at her "Where the hell were you. You don't care for me at all. You didn't even try to meet me once" Rose was completely oblivion of his efforts to meet her.

Mickel replied "I called you umpteen times, you never called back, tried twice to meet you but failed because your mother did not allow me, and I couldn't find my way to barge in. You don't even have modicum of idea what I went through all these days. How could you say all of that?

. "But my mom didn't inform me", she replied looking at him in sheer surprise.

 Further, she revealed that her mother also confiscated her mobile phone, that's why she could not return any of his calls. Now all his questions got answered which were bothering him.

Rose told him about her mother's callous and ostentatious behaviour.

Mickel replied "I implored her to allow me to meet you, but she was unrattled. When I saw her today in the park, I ran to you without wasting a single second, it's overwhelming to finally see you after so much struggle"

Mickel forgot to ask her about her well being. Rose started feeling nausea. He asked her what went wrong? But she was dithering and constantly trying to dodge his interrogation. He t held her hands and insisted her to speak up. She remains silent.

"Let the cat out of the bag", I am all ears" he said.

She started sobbing profusely and spill the beans about her disorder. She said, "I have leukaemia".

He was flabbergasted andwas not able to breathe for a while. He got blank. She anyhow tried to get

him in a control state. She further
added, "My boyfriend also left
me because of this fatal disease."
"Must have been hard to passed
these appalling days". He finally
uttered.
He assured her that, "no matter what it costs,
I am always at your disposal".
Her eyes brimmed with tears and then they both
embraced each other. She concluded, "I have
dearth of time "and asked her to come with him.
She asked for his apology as she spurns his
proposition.
She ensured him to meet the next day on their
rendezvous "I am glad that you came and valued
our friendship. I am so grateful that I have you. I
also want to come with you. But not right now".
Rose said
Mickel replied "I know your mother surely
refrain you from meeting people and specially
me, but you promise me to take care of your
well-being".
"Surely I will, Rose replied"


## Day of their meeting:

Mickel was wearing his favourite attire and
headed out to the park to confess his
emotions again. When he approached to
park, she was not there. He decided to wait
and with a firm determination, he sat on that
bench where they used to sit, discuss their

homework and have their chit chats. Half an hour passed. He saw a couple who were chuckling at each other as if they were watching a comedy show which led him to the nostalgia of bantering and sniggering which they both used to do.

After some time, Rose appeared and surprised him. They both greeted each other with a big smile. He said, "I have been waiting for an hour!!!". She said, "so! Are you about to depart?" "No! never, my conscience doesn't allow, I prefer to wait no matter how much you will delay". He retorted with smile. Soon, they both engaged in verbal confabulations where in Mickel asked about her desires.

"My ardent desire is to get married to someone, enjoy the moments of life with my partner, but at the same time, I don't want to ruin someone's life" She replied sadly. She further added, "I am in a fix Mickel. Presently, I am at that stage of life, when I can collapse anytime. These uncertainties and pessimism encompass me so badly that I couldn't step out and think beyond. And it's so foolish that I am even thinking and pursuing my dreams".

Hearing her he had tears in her eyes. He said to her, "don't think like that, you  have full privilege to marry someone and  pursue your dreams". No one can take your rights".

"Eradicate these stupid and nonsensical thoughts for once, I am not sure if they are feasible or not, I really don't care. All I care is that live your life with absolute confidence and relish every single moment."  He further responded hysterically.

On that note, without any shame or fear I am

proposing you again.  he said, "hey Rose I am insanely in love with you and I am willing to accept your all odds. So, will you marry me, and ready to spend you rest of life with me…. Rose……….". He proposed her blatantly.
There was a hiatus for some fraction of minutes. She said "but Mickel I don't want to
spoil your future. Don't you aware of my disease…
So, I just can't accept your offer as I don't want you to suffer for the rest of your life.!".
She further said, "this time I am just concerned for you, don't take it in a wrong way". "I know I rejected you lately and I am so ashamed knowing the fact that you still care and show profound concern for me.  I have been vacuous recently and I also regret that I showed you my rage that time. And for all that firstly I am awfully sorry for you and secondly, I am tremendously grateful that I collided with you that day." She vocalized remorsefully. Well, Mickel was a patient and active listener, at least when it comes to Rose. After a prolonged discourse, he uttered, "It's alright, you don't need to be sorry. I got you!"
He said, "don't think too much now and yes I am very well cognizant of your vulnerabilities and your stupid disease." He said humorously. "But you need to understand that I made up my mind and with all due respect, I really want to marry and spend the remaining life with you no matter whatever happens." He further added, "I promise to I cater to all your needs, to love you forever. We both are in this together and will come out as winners. We always win as a team.

Don't you remember??Mickel said with brimful eyes. seemed that, a ray of hope beckoned over and Rose couldn't stop snivel listening to him. He said, "Rose I am with you in this and so don't you dare throw yourself in solitude." Now, he succeeded to influence her, and she reluctantly said yes! Then what next! Mickel was on cloud nine…
Rose was whimpering and hugged Mickel by murmuring that "I couldn't fathom you being such a gentleman who unconditionally loves me despite knowing my odds and our future.
 Mickel showed his gratitude towards her. For the next half an hour, they both sat on the same bench. Suddenly it started drizzling which engulfed both of them in delight and happiness. Mickel was brilliant in poetry, he had the ability to knit his feelings gracefully in words. As Mickel and Rose were enjoying the vibes and droplets of rain, Mickel asked her whether she wanted to listen to his poetry. "Yes!", she said.

**He started reciting:**

Rain spreads the sense of tranquillity.
It arrives without notice...
Rain has its own versatility.
And sometimes it returns without justice...

Causes umpteen conundrums.
Though it proves the adequacy of water...

Downpour occurs with outright decorum.

Rain has the privilege to squatter

Parched land invites the rain wholeheartedly.
The petrichor mesmerises unknowingly...

Rain bolsters the crops profoundly.
In return, crops silently obliged to rain
glowingly...


Rain soothes our mind naturally.
It always succeeds in alluring our attention...

It ceases the land purposely.
Anyhow, rain symbolises affection...

Sometimes, rain takes place in insinuation.
And it proves to be deleterious...

Rain clogged the regions which leads to
ruination.
And it seems to be imperious...



*Rain sets the unerring vibes...
The pulchritudinous of rain can't be described...*

Rose said, "Wow!!! Mickel you are stupendous"
After a while, drizzling turned out to downpour.
They both rushed to the shed which was build in
the rightmost corner of the park.
Mickel asked "so is it alright, if we tie our knot

in next week".
Rose said with irresolution, "perfect!", "but what about our parents?"
He said, "why to cross a bridge comes"?
We will clearly discuss this with our families and if they respect our decision, we will seek their blessings otherwise we will elope together and will live happily.
"Well, it seems that you are making castles in the air", she said.
Mickel firmly said "we need
to be intrepid and confident
while talking to our families".
He finally asked her "so are
you ready to go with the
flow!"
She said "Yes and thank you so much, I can't even expect that someone is that much passionate about me. I still impregnates with guilt and worthy of contempt as I reject your proposal earlier" ...
"I am incredibly sorry Mickel", she said whimperingly.
Mickel said, "well to be with you, it's all my pleasure and you need not to be sorry! Please make sure that no matter what comes, you will be happy and ebullient". He further added, "I don't want to see ROSE a distressed and a doomed one."
She said, "OK and now it's too late we should leave now."
Then they both went to their home .

**[Next Day]**

As per the contrivance he made, he headed
towards the Rose house to talk with her mom
about their nuptials. He was quite sure and
cool about his mother in this stuff.
He approached the Rose house. Her mother
Sophia opened the door. She ferociously asked,
"Why are you here?
Mickel said, "I really want to talk something
important, so please let me in!" Then, she
undesirably let him in and he told her about the
significance of matrimony and wedlock. He
was being humorous and loved to annoy
Rose's mother.
"Don't beat about the bush, just get straight
to the point, I don't have time to dodge.
Sophia said".
The whole conservation is being listened by
Rose as she was perpetually gawking both of
them from the stairs.
Mickel then straightforwardly said that "I
want to engage with your lass. She said
"what! Have you lost your all senses"?
He said, "I am completely assured!"
Sophia just turned over in her grave.
 Rose also came down and confess in
front of her mother. Sophia
instantaneously slapped her.
Mickel yelled at Sophia, "what are you doing?
You know what, you haven't been a good
mother at all. You just want to vanquish your
daughter and let me tell you, you are such a
materialistic and callous woman who doesn't
give a damn for Rose. Despite the fact that she is
suffering from leukaemia, you keep on hurting
her!!". He kept on fulminating. It seemed that

how protective Mickel is when it comes to Rose.
 Sophia was losing her patience. She
became restive and immediately propels
him to leave, but he was being
determined and firmed. That was quite
surprising, as she didn't show her
resentment this time. May be, she knew
somehow, that what Mickel said was
true.
 Rose showed hostility towards her mother
which outrageous her. She was ready to leave
her mother to elope with him. Her mother kept
on caterwauling on both of them. But this time
she had enough courage and stood up for herself.
Rose said, "Have you asked your mother?"
He then said, "no worries, we are heading
towards my home as my mom already knew
everything about you since the very beginning
and she is with us." I am quite certain that she
will support us in this too". Then they both
escape to kick off their future life. Finally, they
both approached Mickel's home and met Ava.
She was watering her plants and adoring her
white roses. She saw Mickel and Rose at the
entrance of a gate and welcomed them. She said,
"it's a pleasant surprise and thanked Mickel to
bring Rose". They both looked disturbed. She,
directly asked  Mickel, my son tell me what
bothers you?"
He explained every single event to her. Rose
was sobbing haphazardly. Ava responded
smoothly by consoling Rose, "I understood each
and every pinch of your emotions. I assure both
of you that everything will be alright!". Mickel
took a sign of relief. After a week, they both got

married in the nearby church. Ava assisted them and ensured all the rituals were done properly. Rose enjoyed and relish every single moment of her wedding but she also missed her parents. She was experiencing both pain and happiness.


**[After a year]**

It's been a year now, Mickel never fails to impress and make her happy. He did every single earnest effort to make her smile. However, the leukaemia was being the greatest obstruction in their path of zeal.

They both had an adventurous and undaunted life. Mickel escorted Rose to as many cities as possible as touring the world belonged to one of her dreams. Mickel tried to give her every kind of pleasure and he put all his endeavours to make her fit and fine so that she can get rid of her sufferings.

As we all know that Leukaemia is one of the detrimental diseases which plunges every single person to death and has a pernicious effect on the body. Same was the case here. In the month of February, Rose was persistently facing some complications and Mickel on another side kept on researching the solution and tried to contact the doctors who were expert in this domain. John recommended Dr. Ruth who had an expertise in field of treating cancer. He took Rose to him.

Dr. RUTH inspected her with gentle care. He

could see the abnormal growth of white blood corpuscles in the tissue which kept on reducing her immunity to fight against the fatal disease. Rose's life was at stake. After examining her, Ruth came with disappointment and said "Leukaemia is one of the most lethal disease, it doesn't have any treatment so far. I have also witnessed miracles in some exceptional cases" he took a pause and continued, "But it seems impossible in case of Rose as cells are outgrowing rapidly". He further responded. Mickel was shaken, he begged in front of him and said, "there must be some cure to prevent the outgrowing of cells or anything which we can do to save her life", but the doctor replied negatively.  Rose was also standing there. She tried to stay strong and hold Mickel in her arms. The night turned out to be dreadful for them. Mickel began to lose his hope. Next morning, in anticipation, he woke up and looked at Rose. Rose was still sleeping. He opened his laptop and began to search the preventive measures to stop leukaemia. He did every possible research and met all experts and consultants, but unfortunately, all his efforts were squandered as she was gasping for breath. One day Mickel recalled that its Rose's birthday the net week. He decided to throw a party on her birthday. He invited John, Ava and her some close friends and relatives. Well, it was a surprise for her. He knew her taste. So, he planned accordingly. He also took help from John as he didn't know much about decoration. John managed all the decoration of Rose's birthday and Ava took care of food and stuff. He brought a Gerbera which was her favourite flower. He also bought rivière for her to give her as a birthday present. Rose's birthday was on 20th February, he was very excited, and Rose didn't have the slightest idea of all the planning and surprises that Mickel planned for her. In the morning, he simply wished her and kissed her head. He said, I wanted it to be simple, I don't feel like celebrating or inviting guests. She said, "Okay! Its fine for me!".

In the evening, he sent her to the park with one of her friends, and asked John to complete all the decoration as soon as possible. Ava also joined them. She brought all the food he demanded and Mickel was very punctilious in providing everything that Rose desired. The whole place was illuminating with lights as Rose was fond of lights and colours. Mickel was also ready with Gerbera. All the guests came. Rose didn't return yet. Mickel was busy in the preparation, he lost the track of time and didn't notice that she hadn't arrived the home yet. He got tensed and immediately headed towards the park to look for her. He found that she was sitting in the corner of the park, sobbing and tears rolled down her cheeks. He rushed to her, hugged her tightly and asked, "What happened? Why are you crying and where is your friend?" She responded, "she just left a minute ago." "okay! Let's go home!", he said.

Mickel was feeling low and started weeping as he knew that he was losing her. He said 'Honestly, I didn't even know that I could make

it this far'.
He was numb and decided to spend every single second with her and never leave her alone as her health was deteriorating with a great pace. She was in a morbid state. They both went home. Mickel asked Rose to change and wear the beautiful pink gown that she loved to wear. Rose nodded her head and went upstairs. When she came down, she found it was dark, neither she was able to see anything nor was able to hear any voice. She called Mickel. John switched on the lights and she was amazed to see everything around her. The guests wished her warmly and the party started. Rose was enamored to see the preparations. Mickel and Ava invited her to cut the cake. The party continued till midnight. The guests left happily. Rose said to Mickel, I wanted you to accompany me without asking any question. Mickel smiled and followed her. They were strolling, interlacing their hands into each other pockets. She took him towards the park which was their favourite spot and an umpteen memory to relish. When they reached, Rose began to gasp and reminiscence all the moments which she spent with Mickel there. Their bantering, arguments over silly topics and comforting each other in their hard times and a lot more. It seemed as if she was visualizing all those moments again

They both sat down on the bench where they used to sit earlier. She held his hand and said "please forgive me!" I hate to see you in this condition. I will leave this world soon and today I wanted to disclose one thing to you. She took a slight pause and said, Mickel the truth is that I never had a boyfriend. I just cooked a story. He was dumbstruck and said, "but whyyyyy!" She also confessed that she was attracted towards him from the very first day and I backed out intentionally.

But as my mother was so uncompromising and stringent which always intimidated me, she never allowed me to involve with any guy. To reject your proposal was the most difficult conundrum for me.

I WAS SCARED…. FORGIVE ME
 Rose said.

These revelations left him completely stupefied. He just softly scoffed and then said "it's totally fine and it's not your mistake". She laid down in his lap and extended her apologies and heartfelt gratitude to Mickel for his invariable assistance. Mickel said, Silly girl! I believed you. I never imagined that you lied to me for my sake. I love you a lot….She smiled back with teary eyes. Then, they discussed about their friends, their initial thoughts about each other. They were also listening to their favourite leitmotif and were trying to recall small moments shared by them. She suddenly asked roughly, "Mickel, whom will you marry after my death"?? He replied that I would love to be alone and die widower". He retorted. "Please! Don't discuss such things!!!".

He then said with hesitation, "Can I ask you a question, if you don't mind". "Do ask!" she said.

"When did you come to know about your disease?". He asked. She was wondering that why wouldn't she told him so far. She replied sadly, "well sorry for hurting you again, I found this out recently ……when we met after the party, we had for celebrating a victory, but Sophia knew it since long".

Mickel said, "What???". His temper got aggravated and added, "OMG! I haven't seen a cruel mother like her…, well I am speechless now!".

While Mickel was bursting in anger, Rose started feeling uneasy. Her heartbeat got irregular, and she started breathing heavily. She was sinking down. Mickel's heart was palpitating and a fear of losing the love of his life kept on increasing. Rose was murmuring something which showed her gratefulness towards Mickel. Mickel was humming the bible verses and hoping for some miracle to happen. Rose said, "I wish that I had more time to spend with you, to say thank you. Suddenly there was silence. She left for heavenly abode.

He was completely shattered and bursted in tears. He never intended to marry someone. Though his mother tried to convince him, but he denied. He was truly dedicated and devoted to Rose.

He also wrote one poem for her, expressing their love and addressing his reverence to her.


***Inseparable Bonds***

*Inextricable bonds in the leap of faith...*

*Society haunts them like a wraith...*

*They aren't afraid of thunder...*

*Albeit, both are hoping for wonder...*
*Sitting on the cliff and enjoying the zephyr...*

*Their feelings can't be deciphered...*

*Thinking about each other and both engrossed in carpe diem...*

*The twosome seems very gleam...*

*Both are in love, head over heels*

*But no one can understand how it feels*


Quotidianly, he went to Rose's grave and started conversations. He used to share his all stuff with her which somewhat made him happy…
In a way, he showed his full passion for love and fondness towards Rose, and for the rest of his life, he continued his life as a widower, though many girls came across, but he chose to spend with the soul of Rose.

He is emblematic of commitment who showcases his love aesthetically.
**Love is irreplaceable.**


This story is quintessential and completely justifies the term, **"Meant for each other!!!"**

# The End

# MEANT FOR EACH OTHER

## ABOUT THE BOOK

They met they parted their ways

As destiny for them had a different play

It 's not just a lv story...

A demure innocent girl and introvert boy, one fine day they came across each other and their fate changed forever.

A tale about their enchanting journey which they meant to complete together

Lets find out were they able to do so?

An eternal love story--------